GHOSTS

OF

DES MOINES COUNTY,
IOWA

by
Bruce Carlson

Quixote Press
1854 345th Avenue, Wever, Iowa 52658
1-800-571-2665

\* \* \* \* \* \* \* \* \* \* \*

Although the author has exhaustively researched
all sources to ensure the accuracy and com-
pleteness of the information contained in this
book, he assumes no responsibility for errors,
inaccuracies, omissions or any inconsistency
herein. Any slights of people or organizations
are unintentional. Readers should consult an
attorney or accountant for specific applica-
tions to their individual publishing ventures.

QUIXOTE
PRESS

Bruce Carlson                    Printed
Wever, Iowa 52658                in the
                                 U.S.A.

When I wrote GHOSTS OF DES MOINES COUNTY
back in the early 1980's, I banged it
out on my old Underwood typewriter.

Since those days, a lot has changed.
I've written another hundred or so
books, and the typewriter is pretty much
retired.

This new edition now in 2004 is exactly
the same as that old one from the 80's.
The illustration on page 55 is kind of
faded and washed out, but that's OK.
I've gotten kind of faded and washed
out, myself, since then.

Bruce Carlson

## DEDICATION

I want to dedicate this book to my wife,
Marilyn Carlson.  She has put up with countless nights of my banging away on my old
Underwood typewriter while writing this book.
She expected, and certainly deserved, some
respite from that after a previous book I
wrote.  But, Ah, rest was not to come.  She
had to suffer through this one, also.

The author wants to express his appreciation to the many people who have been of invaluable help by sharing family records and personal experiences. Without that help, this book would be only a front and a back cover.

THE BURLINGTON AREA WRITERS' CLUB has been very helpful in offering suggestions and constructive critisms as well as sharing its enthusiasm and support.

# TABLE OF CONTENTS

# FOREWORD

All the residents of Des Moines County are
well aware of things and places like the
Mississippi, Highway #34, and Burlington.
Most of them have at least heard of Flint
Creek, Oakville, Augusta, and Dodgeville.

But how many know about Sherfey's Glen, the
house with the cold spot, the haunted fairy
ring, the living doll, or the man whose
partner on his cross-cut saw was his brother's
solitary arm?

Bruce Carlson's book, <u>GHOSTS OF DES MOINES
COUNTY</u> is an immensely readable collection
of ghost stories from this southeastern
Iowa county.

There will undoubtedly be a few readers who
are able to put this book down before fin-
ishing it. However, I don't think there
will be many who can do it. Readers will
be hooked on this book all the way through
to the end of the last chapter.

Professor Phil Hey<br>
Briar Cliff College<br>
Sioux City, Iowa

# PREFACE

The reader will find, in this book, a collection of tales about ghosts in Des Moines County.

The events described in this volume cover the period from before the Civil War until, and including, 1986. They are, however, not in chronological, or any other order. Each story is a separate chapter, unrelated to any of the others.

Whenever possible, diligent effort was made to confirm these stories by getting information from other sources. That was, of course, not always possible. Ghost stories are often known to only a very small number of people.

The reader must appreciate the fact that, with only a couple of exceptions, none of these stories have ever been published. Some of them could cause embarrassment to living people today. Because of that, some of the stories use fictitious names. In those cases, it should be understood that any similarity between those names and actual people, living or dead, is purely coincidental.

The author hopes that this book will serve to document some of the tales heretofore only handed down by word of mouth. They are part of the heritage of Des Moines County and deserve to be preserved.

It is emphasized that these are in the nature of folk tales. If the reader is looking for sensational stories of blood and gore, he won't find them here. If he is looking for stories with a heavy religious orientation, he had better look elsewhere. If, however, some pleasant (and hopefully, accurate) accounts of ghosts who have resided here in Des Moines County appeal to you, I invite you to spend a few hours with me in GHOSTS OF DES MOINES COUNTY.

# CHAPTER I

## THE WEIGHT ON THE BED

an a father care to the point of terror?  Can he have been so close to his children that even after he dies, his grown daughter can feel him reaching out to her?  Can he reach with such realism that she becomes petrified with fear?

Perhaps so.

Perhaps that is what happened in Burlington on South Marshall Street back in 1978.  At age 40 Myrna lay in bed very pregnant and was very tired of laying there.  She had been bedfast for a month and had four more to go.  Perhaps had she felt bad, her having been sentenced to that bed by her doctor would have been more bearable.  Her pregnancy and the clots in her legs made it all necessary, however.  In spite of her boredom, she felt relatively good physically.  This made the time pass slowly.  Her room in the basement wasn't well lit during the day so there was little difference between day and

night. She made her own day by turning the
light on.

Myrna said; "I sure got sick of laying there."

"I'll bet you did." I replied.

"It was dark when it happened, but I was wide
awake. What I went through was not a dream.
I was fully awake and knew what was happening.

"It was mid-August, and as I lay there in the
dark, I couldn't help but think of all the fun
summer things I could have been doing the next
day. But, no, I had to lie in that bed.

"Suddenly I felt Jimbo, the dog, jump up on the
foot of the bed. He did that on occasion but
always got into lots of trouble for it."

"Maybe he didn't know you were there." I said.

"Oh, he knew! Besides that, he knew I never
let him jump up on any of the furniture.

"The impact of his landing and his weight on
the foot of the bed was not a bit comfortable.
I had surgical stockings on plus several layers
of bedclothes. I sure didn't need a dog laying
there.

"I hollered out:  'Jimbo, get down!  Knowing Jimbo, I knew he would immediately jump back down on the floor.  The weight on the bed remained.  I was able to shout out;  'Jimbo, get down!' one more time before the full realization hit me."

"What realization?"

"I realized that was not Jimbo!  There is no way he would have stayed.

"I tried to scream, but I was so afraid that not a sound came out.  It was like being in one of those old silent movies.  I could move, but I was struck dumb with fear."

I asked Myrna what she thought it was on the bed.  She went on to tell me that she was so gripped with terror she couldn't even think of that right then.

"Finally, after what seemed forever with that terrible weight on the foot of the bed, I managed to reach over to turn the light on.  Just as I switched it on, the weight disappeared. I looked down at the foot of the bed and saw nothing."

I asked, "What do you think it was?"

"I am convinced it was my father warning me of problems to come.  I felt that to be true as soon as I recovered from that terrible experience.  It was so much like Dad to try to help, reaching out to me even from the grave.  He had been dead three years by then.  Dad was always so concerned about us kids, and I was his favorite.  I'm totally convinced to this day that it was him."

"Did a problem follow that experience?  Did he really have anything to warn you about?"

"There sure was," she replied.  "I had my child soon after that in my eighth month of pregnancy. He was so little, only three pounds and four ounces.  We almost lost him.  In addition, the delivery had been rough on me.  It was, in fact, touch and go for me for awhile."

As I sat and listened to Myrna's story and saw her very obviously strong feelings showing through, I had no reason to doubt her at all. Perhaps it is true.  Perhaps a father can love too much.

# CHAPTER II

## KISHAUNA'S FRIEND

When I pulled into the Larry and Karla Andreas' home halfway between Mediapolis and Highway #99, I saw Karla in the drive.

I don't really know how I knew it was Karla. She just looked like a girl named Karla.

She also looked like a girl who wouldn't have had any experience with ghosts. Perhaps it was the bright October day. Maybe it was her fresh Midwestern farm-girl appearance. She just didn't have the look of someone who had crossed paths with the supernatural. I knew, however, that she had. A friend of hers from near Kingston had told me that.

Karla proved to be a likeable and friendly young housewife who kind of looked at me sideways when I asked her to share her ghost story. I could see her thinking: "Who is this guy barging in like this asking about my ghost friend?"

Sideways glances notwithstanding, she sat down the eggs she was holding and told me about a two-year period in her life in 1982 and 1983. It took place in a house she and Larry were renting then.

Karla's embarrassment seemed to evaporate as it became apparent that I wasn't going to laugh at her.

"We were living in that house and had some really strange experiences."

"What kind of experiences?", I asked.

"Well, mostly it was a matter of feelings we had rather than particular things that happened."

Karla told me about the feelings that she and others had while standing at the foot of the stairs.

"We just could not stand there with our backs to the stairs. We had to face them."

"Why?"

"I don't know. It was just an awful feeling if we turned our backs on those stairs."

As Karla talked on, she touched on several strange happenings in that house. Her telling about the loud thumps from somewhere in the house whenever she swore, came almost as a confession.

"Thumps, you say?"

"Yes, they were loud thumps or raps. I don't know where they came from there in the house, but that is what they were."

"What else happened?"

"Well, there was the matter of what I, at
first, thought was my daughter Kishauna's
playing with the toys in her room. I remember one time I was downstairs relaxing
and listening to Kishauna playing up there.
I could very clearly
hear those toys bang-
ing around and all that
laughing and giggling.
I was nine months preg-
nant at the time and
with Kishauna being
only a year and a half
old, I enjoyed the chance
to relax and listen to
her having fun. After a while, I went up to
get her and was shocked to find that she was
sound asleep. The noise lasted until just
before I went into her room. When I opened
the door, she was really asleep.

"But couldn't she have jumped into bed when
she heard you coming?"

"A one and a half year old isn't that good at
fooling her mother. She was really really
fast asleep. And it happened other times
after that. I'd hear all that play noise

19

and find her in a deep sleep when I went into her room.

"There were other little things. That door into the spare bedroom upstairs was super hard to open because the house had settled and the door would bind and had worn a deep groove in the floor. It would drag so bad that we had to lift up hard on the knob in order to open it."

"Well, what happened to the door?" I asked.

"Lots of times it would be wide open when we both knew we hadn't been in there. It was a spare bedroom, and we just didn't have any reason to go into it. I'd clean in there, but not very often. It just didn't get dirty very much.

"Another thing was the footsteps coming up the stairs at night. We'd hear them come up and then go down the hallway. You know, after awhile you kind of get used to that sort of thing.

"I always felt the ghost was a woman. I don't know why, I just sensed it to be a woman. I even had the impression that she was concerned about Kishauna and wanted to protect her. That's kind of neat, you know. Maybe I figured it was a woman because a previous tenant had seen a woman and a child at the upstairs window one day. The lady rushed in to find out who was in her home and found no one.

"Then there was the deal with the beer."

"The beer?"

About this time Larry pulled into the drive-
way. Feeling that an explanation was in order,
I introduced myself and told him about my
interest in ghost stories.

"I was getting ready to tell him about the
beer story. Why don't you?"

"Okay, I'll tell it.

"I had brought a six-pack home from town. It
was late and I'd worked hard all day so decided to down one before turning in. I opened a
can and put the other five in the refrigerator. It was one of those six-packs with the
plastic ring holder. Karla had just gone to
bed. I drank the beer, set the can on the
table, and turned in, too. Come morning, we
went down to the kitchen for some breakfast.
There on the table was that empty can. Inside the refrigerator were four full ones and
one empty one."

"An empty one?"

"It sure was."

"Sure you didn't have two beers that night
before?"

"No way. I drank just one and went to bed.
Besides, I never would have put the empty
one back in the refrig."

I suggested the possibility that Kishauna
might have been messing around with the beer.

"There is no way that could be. At a year
and a half, she couldn't even open that door,
much less get a beer can open.

21

"Well, anyway, we decided to give the old ghost another chance. That second day I drank a beer, leaving three in the refrigerator. I set the empty can down on the kitchen table, and Karla and I went to bed together. We got up and went down to the kitchen the following morning together. There was that empty can there on the table and inside the refrigerator were......"

I was waiting for the next word. Would there be only two cans? Would there be the three left? In my anticipation of that next word, I had failed to puff on my cigar and it went out. Apparently, Larry was a born storyteller. He chose that moment to kick the tire there on the pickup and to tuck in his shirttail.

Good grief! How many cans were left? I was busy searching my pockets for a match to get that cigar going again.

"......only two left and an empty can in there."

At this point I observed that a ghost that would eat liver or rutabaga out of the refrigerator would be halfway tolerable, but a beer-drinking one was kind of serious business. Larry agreed and told me that he hollered out a general announcement to the effect that he'd put up with no more of that foolishness. Reflecting a moment, he corrected himself. "Actually, I think I said I'd appreciate it if there were no more of that foolishness."

Apparently Larry's announcement took root somewhere in the recesses of that old house. That was the last of that sort of foolishness.

## CHAPTER III

## THE SECRET GHOST

his was to have been a ghost story.
I guess it really is all right. In
a way, though, the ghost is almost
incidental. But why did, in fact,
how could the family members keep
the secret from each other?

The Wilcox house there on South Gunnison in
Burlington was built in the late 1800's.
The six-member family lived there over a
twenty-year period. By the time they left,
the family had grown to nine.

The story of that ghost on South Gunnison
includes many of the elements of other
haunted house stories here in Des Moines
County. The unique element is the response
of the individuals in the family. For various reasons, each person kept his experience
secret from the others.

The wife, Mrs. Wilcox, saw things but told
only her husband. Neither he nor the boys
saw anything. The girls all saw and heard

much more than they wanted and said nothing
to anyone.

In spite of these pretensions of normalcy,
there were lots of unexplainable things going
on in that house.

There were those faces peering in at the girls
in their upstairs bedroom.  At least some of
those were known cases of Peeping Toms.  Mrs.
Wilcox, who was telling me the story, dismissed
those with the observation that;  "You know, a

 bunch of teenaged girls will
attract a certain number of
that kind."  Perhaps most,
or even all, of those faces
belonged to very mortal
owners.  That front porch
made a handy perch for those
birds.

Those "Peeping Toms" that were seen peering <u>out</u>
of the window were something else, of course.
It has to be conceded that a reverse Peeping
Tom is a new twist.

"Faces at the windows weren't the only ones.
Jane was in the basement when a face appeared
to her.  It was that of an old man, and it was
surrounded by a ring of light.  It was suspended in the air and was about six feet off
the floor."

"What did she do?"

Mrs. Wilcox replied, "I only know what she told
me years later.  She said not a word about what
she did at the time.  Neither did I know until
years later that the same thing happened inside
the girls' bedroom.  All that I knew back then

was that the girls wouldn't stop pestering us until their Dad and I traded rooms with them.

"Then there were the times that the name of one or the other of us would be called out."

"Did this ever happen when only one person was in the house?"

My question so struck Mrs. Wilcox that she never did get around to answering it. The idea of only one person being in the house with a family of nine! My question probably showed such a lack of familiarity with the comings and goings of a large family that it didn't even deserve an answer.

"I wonder which of all these things affected the kids the most?" I said.

"Well, first of all, it wasn't the kids at all. It was the girls only. Like I said, neither Jim nor the boys ever saw anything. Secondly, the most upsetting thing was something else. It was the cold spot."

"The cold spot? What do you mean by the cold spot?"

"It was just that. It was a cold spot a bit over halfway up the stairs. It was always colder than the area above or below it. The girls used to dash up and down the stairs through it rather than to linger there."

My speculation about a window draft kind of trailed off as she explained that there was no window along or near the stairway.

Mrs. Wilcox continued, "I thought it was

just teenage exuberance as those girls rushed up and down those stairs that way."

"But didn't you feel the cold spot?"

"I sure did. It was awful!"

"I don't understand. Didn't you talk about it?"

"No. Other than my talking to Jim about my experiences in that house, nobody said anything to anyone."

"That's amazing," I commented. "Why not?"

"Jim and I agreed not to tell the kids for fear of upsetting them. I kind of think Jim's real reason was to hide the fact, from the kids, that their mother had one oar out of the water. My purpose was to keep it from them for their own peace of mind.

"It wasn't until that family reunion years later when we got to talking about that house. The kids were all grown and had left home. One of the girls confessed to having seen a face suspended in the bedroom. From that point on, it was a general confession hour. Every one of the girls had been harboring a secret about things she had seen and heard."

"Why in the world didn't they say anything at the time?"

"As we talked about it that day, it became very obvious that all the girls had done the same thing. Each one was afraid that to share her experience meant she had to face the fact that those things really happened. That was simply

more than they could do.  It was fear of
fear itself that kept the girls from telling each other or us about what had happened.  I guess it was some kind of defense
mechanism."

"That's amazing!"

"You had better believe it was.  I'm sorry
now that it worked out that way.  Had we
been more honest with each other we could
have seen that cursed house for what it was
and left a lot sooner.  There was no warmth
or sense of 'home' in that place.  None of
us liked it.  No number of curtains, cutsey
plaques, or anything else could warm that
house up.  I'm glad we finally left when we
did."

"Did the kids feel that way, too?"

"The girls did.  In fact, Judy was born in
that house and lived there until she was 15.
At 17, she simply could not remember what
the interior of the place looked like."

"Was it a scary and spooky kind of house?"
I asked.

"No, not really.  There
was lots of stress, but
it wasn't spooky.  In
fact, the girls found
an old trunk up in the
attic and played up
there a lot with that
old thing."

"A trunk?"

"Yes, but there wasn't anything exciting in it; only some old clothes and papers."

"I would have thought they would have been a-fraid to go up there."

"No, they weren't.  I figured out later that almost everything strange that had happened was either in the basement or on the second floor.  Perhaps the attic was kind of a refuge."

How many haunted houses have a dingy old at-tic as a safe haven from ghosts?  There is no end to the surprises in this ghosting business.

# CHAPTER IV

## THE TWO AT THE GATE

ot all ghost stories are long ones.

Lillian Schulte from near Dodgeville told me of one her father, James McGloughlin, passed on to her many, many years ago.

It seems that two boys were tarrying at the gate of Old Stone Cemetery near Dodgeville when they heard, "Two for you and two for me; and don't forget the two at the gate."

The boys were reported to have moved out right smartly.

# CHAPTER V

## THE SHY GHOST

ome ghosts are scary. Some are downright terrifying. Old Joash never did get his act together enough to be either one. He was always just a plain pest. He was like a gnat, always 'abuzzing around your head. Gnats don't bite, scratch, kick or sting. They are just pesky. So it was with Joash.

Joash is one of the few mobile ghosts in Des Moines County. He's been around to several homes in Huron Township. His home base has, at least for a long time, been the Burton house there in the township. The Burton farm has been in the family for a long, long time, so Joash is assumed to be a relative. Like other relatives, he could be a bit of a pain in the neck and show up at inconvenient times. He generally made his presence known by kicking on the door. No efforts to see Joash were ever successful. Every time they would answer the door he'd be gone. When the Burtons remodeled their home, they moved the front door a few feet to the north.

This kind of threw Joash for a loop. He'd continue to kick at where the door used to be. His penchant for habit even included the time of day. He'd generally show up at 7:00 P.M.

One evening at the regular hour in 1971, Joash was up to his habit of kicking around where the door used to be. One of the older members of the family was short on patience that day anyway. He hollered out, "Oh, go away, Joash; you're making too much noise." That so hurt the feelings of the Scourge of Huron Township that he didn't come back for a long time. When he did, he changed his time to 9:00. Apparently, he was in hope the old folks would be in bed by then and maybe the younger ones would be more hospitable.

Several theories have been advanced as to why Joash was always banging there at the house. Popular ones were that he was a relative home from the war or the Gold Rush. Another persistent one has been that he isn't a relative at all, but a stagecoach driver needing help with an ailing horse.

While Joash still kicks with equal vigor these days, he shows up less frequently and stays around for shorter periods. Apparently, he is spending a lot more time doing whatever ghosts do when they aren't pestering decent law-abiding citizens.

# CHAPTER VI

## THE QUIET WOMAN

uth White lives in Davenport now but she used to live near the High School on Marietta Street in Burlington, and that is where Ruth's story took place.

She was in the ninth grade back in 1965. Her bedroom was a spacious one on the second floor of that old rambling house there on Marietta. Ruth was sitting at the mirror of her vanity setting her hair. Looking past her own image in the mirror she was surprised to see an old lady standing behind her.

"Was the image of this woman clear, or was it like a mist or cloud?" I asked.

"She was just as clear as if she were anyone else standing there. I turned around quickly and there she was, just as in the mirror. She was dressed in a shawl-like garment with a hood that was halfway up on her head. I was impressed at how blue that shawl was. It was not of a fine cloth, however. It was a very coarse material. She was standing only about eight feet away so I could see her face clearly."

"Was the light on? Was it day or night?"

"It was in the evening, but there were several lights in my room and most of them were on. The light was perfectly adequate.

"The woman looked at me for a moment and then walked backwards into my closet whose door was open behind her."

"What was in the closet at the time?"

"It was full of clothes, more or less jam full. You know how teenage girls are, don't you?

"I was surprised to find that I was not a bit afraid. I got up and hurried over to that closet. There was nothing in there but those clothes and assorted junk."

"Did you ever see her again?"

"Yes, twice more. The second time I was in my room again, home from school with the flu, and the only one in the house. I was studying or reading in an easy chair I had. I looked up and there she stood in front of me. She had the same clothes on and looked very, very real; just like anyone else would. She raised her arms up and held her hands out to me, palms forward.

"This time I spoke to her. I asked her for her name. She walked a couple of steps toward me, still with her hands out. Then abruptly she stepped sideways and stepped into that same closet."

"Were you afraid that time?", I asked.

"No."

I asked Ruth if anyone else in the house had ever seen anything strange.

"Yes, I asked my mother if she had. She told me she had, but she wouldn't give me any details.

"Then there was the third and last time I saw the woman. It was shortly before we moved away. My mother and I were coming down the stairs with the family dog tagging along. At the foot of the stairs, there was a large living room off to the right and a dining room to the left. We were almost all the way down to the bottom when I glanced into the living room. There stood the same woman. I immediately turned to my mother who, at that same moment, also saw her. Without saying anything, we continued down the two or three remaining steps and stopped. As soon as we did, the dog looked into the living room and barked excitedly. Like many dogs, his bark sometimes meant certain things. He had one sound for a hunger bark, another to be let in and so forth. He also had one for when there was a stranger in the house. It was that bark he was using as we stood there. The dog was looking at the same spot where we could see the woman standing.

"Suddenly, without warning, the woman seemed to quickly recede in space and was gone."

"What did you do? Did you discuss it?"

"Only briefly, Mother didn't want to talk about it."

In 1974 or 1975, Ruth went back to that house and asked the occupants if they had ever seen any strange things in the house. They said they had indeed, but were very firm in their refusal to talk about it.

So, who was the woman on Marietta Street? To this day Ruth White has no idea, and her mother won't talk about it.

# CHAPTER VII

## A GIRL NAMED RANDY

hen I went to that large old house on South Hill in Burlington on the appointed day, I was met at the door by Mrs. James.

My first impression was that she was less enthused about meeting with me than I would have hoped. Perhaps my coming a bit early was an inconvenience. Perhaps she had second thoughts about revealing circumstances and events that had been kept secret up 'til now.

Within a few minutes, however, what I had felt to be aloofness dissolved in the friendliness and hospitality she and Mr. James showed me.

There was little hint in the house that it was an old one. The decor was bright and airy. The Jameses had done extensive remodeling and had furnished the house to create a very contemporary, yet homey atmosphere.

Neither was there anything there to hint that this very likeable couple had raised a family

of seven children in the house. A person does
not usually associate a ghost with a house full
of seven noisy kids. Perhaps, on the other
hand, this was appropriate because the ghost
hasn't been of the shy and retiring type.
"Randy", the ethereal member of the family is
a busy ghost. She leads a rather hectic life,
or whatever it is that ghosts lead.

I guess it should be explained how Randy got a
boy's name when, in fact, she is very much a
pretty little girl. The family gave her that
name somewhat arbitrarily. Numerous unexplainable events were credited to the work of Randy.
She was so busy and so involved in the affairs
of the family that they really felt compelled
to name her.

It was the James' son, Brian, that found out
Randy was a girl. Brian was 14 when he saw her
and was able to give a good description of her to
his folks. To fully tell the story, however, we
have to back up 13 years to when Brian was less
than a year old.

> It all started that day when Brian was
> but a toddler. Mrs. James had gone up
> into the attic to explore that inacces-
> sible place in that house that they had
> acquired a short time earlier. It was
> a bit of a chore to get up there since
> a stairway had never been built. There
> was only a trapdoor that required drag-
> ging a ladder up to the top of the stairs.
> Mrs. James had done just that and had gone
> up into that dark and dusty place to clean
> it.
>
> The attic was, and still is, unfinished.
> A person has to balance himself on the

floor joists for fear of falling in
through the plastered ceiling below.
She gathered up some old picture frames
on that small floored area around the
trapdoor. She swept the floor and returned to the kitchen; fully armed
with a bunch of those old frames.

She had had a fancy for old pictures
for some time and studied her find before pitching most of the old photos
and keeping the antique frames.

She momentarily debated whether or not
to throw away one of the portraits.
It was a portrait of a girl about five
years old. She was wearing an ornate
and old-fashioned dress with pleats
down the front. Her hair was a strik-
ing blond. She was a pretty little
girl with large blue eyes. Unfortunately, that photo went into the trash
with many of the rest of them. Mrs.
James was considerably more interested
in her plans to refinish those frames
than she was in saving many of those
dusty old photos. She did wonder
later why she didn't keep that particular one of the little girl.

Meanwhile, Brian played there on the
floor on the other side of that large
kitchen as his mother fussed over those
portraits.

The next 13 years were filled with all the
incidents that led to the family being aware
that they had a ghost in the house. It was
during that time that they named "him" Randy.
Brian's experience at age 14 happened in his

bedroom upstairs. He was tired and had lain down for a nap. Suddenly the house was filled with terrified screams coming from that room. Mr. and Mrs. James rushed up to see what was wrong. They found a screaming Brian sitting on the edge of his bed. His eyes were large and tear-filled, fixed on a low bookcase at the far wall.

"She is laughing at me. She's teasing me and staring at me!

"She is going to get me. Can't you see her?"

As Mrs. James started to walk toward the book-case, he frantically stopped her.

"She'll get you, too! She'll get you too! She'll get you too!"

Their efforts to comfort Brian led them to take him downstairs and hold him for awhile. He eventually calmed down, but never again would he enter that room alone.

Brian was a boy who tended to ignore unpleasant inci-dents. As expected, he had nothing to say about the episode in his room for a long time. Several months went by before he brought the subject up again. He asked, "Mom, why do you call our ghost 'Randy'? It isn't a boy. It's a girl."

"How do you know that, Brian?"

Brian then described that figure he had seen

months earlier. Mrs. James had already dismissed Brian's experience as a result of an
over-active teen-age imagination. Her listening to his account of that little girl he
had seen was little more than an indulgence
on her part. That is, it was until she realized that he was describing, in full detail,
a child of the exact appearance of that one
in the portrait she had thrown away years
before. That was when Brian was but a toddler
across the kitchen from where she was looking
at those old photos from the attic.

It was at this point that Mrs. James felt that
what Brian saw was indeed the ghost, and that
ghost was of the beautiful little girl in that
old photo. Mr. James was yet unconvinced. He
steadfastly remained the family skeptic. He
knew that it was simply a teenager's imagination and the unwarranted acceptance of this
foolishness by his wife. Randy was soon to
puncture that all too neat theory of Mr.
James's.

It happened one night. The couple had gone to
bed and were lying there discussing the multi-
tude of the daily events incidental to the
raising of a large family. Suddenly, they
felt a cold mist-like presence in the room.
It wasn't one of those "Is it me, or is it
really suddenly cold in here?" type of things.
It was cold. It was intense, and it was real!

The Jameses talked about that quite awhile
that night. Finally, Mr. James started to
drift off to sleep. This was a luxury denied Mrs. James. She remained fully awake,
still concerned about that cold mist. She
turned to him to get through his drowsiness
in order to ask a question. Failing to get

a response, she lay back down.  As she was
doing so, she turned her head toward her edge
of the bed.

There stood Randy!

Randy was no more than one and a half to two
feet from Mrs. James.  She stood there in the
same dress she wore in that photo;  the same
one young Brian had described so vividly
earlier.  Mrs. James was amazed at the beauty
of the child.  She could see her clearly.  It
was as if it were a real child standing in that
bedroom.  There was none of that formlessness
or fuzziness about Randy.  She was crystal clear
and an absolutely beautiful girl of about five
years old.  She stood there in that pleated
dress.  There were those same large eyes and
blond hair that Brian had seen.

With her eyes riveted on that little girl, Mrs.
James reached over to shake her husband awake.
It was only with considerable grumbling and
complaining that Mr. James reluctantly rolled
over to demand an explanation for being so
rudely awakened.  That was his last act as a
skeptic.  He too saw that Randy was really
there.  What he saw was the same as what his
startled wife did.  Their descriptions matched.  As if he were being punished for his
earlier disbelief, Mr. James' look was but
fleeting.  Randy disappeared very quickly.
That was the last time she was to appear to
the James family except in unclear and nebu-
lous ways.  Later two of the girls saw Randy,
but not clearly.

Like these later two appearances, there were
other events that were probably the work of
Randy.  There were the sounds of someone

walking when the family member hearing them was alone in the house. There were unexplained losses of items, followed by their reappearance. There were the openings and closings of doors without apparent cause.

One could speculate that some of these were of natural origin. The footsteps could have been those of an intruder. The openings and closings of doors seen by family members could be argued to be the result of the sleepiness common to people who get up in the middle of the night for a trip to the bathroom. Items often turn up missing and then later are found right where they belong.

There are a couple of other incidents that can't be explained away, however. For example, there was the incident of the gifts in the attic.

> The gifts in the attic were disconcerting at first, but with time and repeated occurance, they became almost welcome.

That cleaning that Mrs. James did up in the attic was not the last time she had to do that. Later, she had occasion 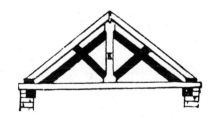 to look up there. She was shocked to find a box setting on that small patch of floor where the frames had been. That box had not been there before!

Subsequent checks of that small area in the attic yielded more boxes, a candle holder, another picture frame, etc. On one occasion, Mrs. James painted the ceiling and trapdoor, thus sealing the crack. The next trip into the attic necessitated breaking that paint seal. That trip also provided a new gift. One of the more interesting gifts from the attic is a bracelet with a mustard seed embedded in a transparent pendent.

Each time that area was cleaned well so as to be sure that everything was gone. That trapdoor was the only entrance to the attic. Apparently, Randy is as generous as she is beautiful.

The stereo affair is also totally unexplainable.

Mrs. James was alone one day cleaning the house. In a bedroom upstairs she plugged the vacuum cleaner into a receptacle. To do that, she found it necessary to unplug a stereo.

The kids had that thing plugged in and the speakers positioned around the room, trailing their wires. While there, Mrs. James gathered up those speakers and stacked them neatly by the player so people wouldn't be tripping over them.

She left the stereo unplugged, the speakers neatly stacked, and closed the door behind her; returning to the first floor. Since she was alone in the house, it came as a shock to hear that stereo playing as soon as she got to the bottom of the stairway. Upon opening the door to investigate she found the speakers scattered around, the stereo plugged in and playing along quite merrily.

Who was the beautiful little girl in the photo? Why did she roam the recesses of that large old house? Would the course of events in the James' house have been any different if Mrs. James had saved that portrait, rather than discarding it?

Perhaps the only one who knows is that little girl with the large blue eyes and the long golden hair.

# CHAPTER VIII

## THE SHEET BLANKET INCIDENT

he Dawson family live in a hundred-year-old house on South Ballard in West Burlington. This was the area known as Shopton back in the early 1880's when the house was built.

When I met the family at their home, I was told that they didn't have much to tell me about ghosts. They both felt that maybe their story about their daughter, Nancy, wasn't interesting enough.

With that, they went on to spin a fascinating story about her.

I didn't meet Nancy that evening. She was off doing whatever pretty seventeen-year-old girls do while the rest of us talk about ghost stories. From a photo, however, it was obvious that she is a vivacious young lady with a sparkle in her eyes. The articles and photos taped on the refrigerator door testify to her interests and accomplishments in a variety of athletics. Her parents described a typical

47

teen-age girl with the normal teen-aged penchant
for hamburgers, music, etc.

Nancy's story took place in 1977 when she was
eight years old.  She, like many other children,
was prone to wandering around in her sleep.
Perhaps this was because she knew her room upstairs was haunted.  Her older sister was also
convinced of that.  Neither Nancy nor her sister had ever seen a ghost in that room, but
they knew there was something there.  An old man
had died many years earlier in the adjacent room
where the girls' brother slept, but it was the
girls' room about which they had that distinct
feeling.

Nancy's dedication to having a neat bed was
less than total.  Perhaps that is being a bit
charitable.  The brutal truth is that at eight
years of age, she had never made a bed in her
life.  The bed had been made that night, however before she climbed into it.  Her mother
was confident of that because she had made it
for Nancy.

The nights were cool at the time, so Mrs. Dawson had put flannel sheet blankets on the bed
for warmth.  As the Dawsons retired for the
evening, there was nothing to indicate that
this night would be any different than any
other.

During the wee hours of the night, the couple
heard a noise coming from the living room.  Upon investigating they found Nancy fitfully
sleeping in their large beanbag chair.  She had

her sheet blanket with her and was wrapped in it there on the beanbag.

Mrs. Dawson said, "We woke her so she could go back up to her room. That was really something!"

"It sure was, we'd never seen anything like that before!" echoed Mr. Dawson.

"What happened?" I asked.

Mrs. Dawson went on to explain; "As soon as she was awake, she swung her head around and stared at the doorway leading upstairs. The really strange thing was the look in her eyes and on her face. She looked different than we had ever seen her before. She looked like a total stranger to us. We'll never forget how she looked. You know, it's kind of a shock to have your own daughter appear to be a stranger."

The Dawsons went on to tell that as soon as Nancy looked away from that stairway, her appearance was back to normal. The racing hearts of her parents weren't, however. The Dawsons were pretty agitated, having seen how their daughter looked. They thought it best not to talk to her about that. They simply urged her to go back to her room. Still upset over her countenance of a couple of minutes earlier, both parents went to her room with her.

In that room everything was pretty much normal except for one important difference. The bed was made. It was perfectly made without a fold out of place.

Mrs. Dawson turned to Nancy and asked her if

she had made the bed. It was a bit of a rhe-
torical question. She knew that her daughter
did not make it and was incapable of making
it. There was no one else in the house that
could have slipped in and made it.

"I pulled back the bedclothes. They were the
same ones I had put on it, except that one of
the sheet blankets was not there."

"It was clutched in the arms of Nancy standing
nearby." said Mr. Dawson.

Who made that bed? And why? Did the old man
who had died in the next room have anything to
do with it? Maybe so. That room next door, in

fact, has a story of its own. The
Dawsons had bought their house
back in 1962. They used that bedroom where the old man had died.
The ceiling fixture was turned on
and off the normal number of times
in those 24 years. The interesting
thing is that the light bulb in
that room had never been changed
in all those years. It could be
said that any ghost who could keep
that light bulb burning for 24
years, could certainly make a bed.

# CHAPTER IX

## LUCINDA

It comes as no surprise that the ghost of Stoney Hollow should be one associated with a love story.

Stoney Hollow is a truly beautiful series of ravines and high bluffs six miles north of Burlington. The creek wanders through there making lots of twists and turns. It's almost as if it is reluctant to leave the hollow. Those cool deep ravines offer welcome respite on a hot August day.

In fact, the love story of Stoney Hollow ended in tragedy on a hot August evening many many years ago. The best estimate is that it was in the late 1870's or the early 1880's.

The daughter of a local farmer was courted by many of the boys in the neighborhood. The more daring of them asked to be allowed to see her. The rest simply suffered through the pangs of love unspoken and unreturned. Beautiful young Lucinda had skin the hue of an acorn and long hair the color of the jet

black feathers of the breast of the blackbird.
Like those feathers, it was so black as to be
almost metallic blue.

Lucinda's father knew that his fine farm along
with his daughter's beauty would enable him to
arrange a very advantageous marriage for her.
He had visions of an exceedingly generous dowry
or even the opportunity to combine, through marriage, his attractive farm with another of equal
or better quality.

His dream ran headlong into trouble.  Trouble
came in the form of a local suitor whose family
enjoyed neither prestige or property.  The farmer could amost ignore that annoyance until he
learned that Lucinda and this young ne'er-do-well
were having rendezvous there in Stoney Hollow,
then called Sherfey's Glen.  He discovered that
each of the two young lovers would walk along
the hill tops to meet there at a secret place
in the glen.

Lucinda was ordered to stop seeing the young
man.  That confrontation simply led her and
her lover to move their planned elopement up
a few weeks.  They conspired to meet a couple
days later and then leave together.  He would

bring a horse and
buggy and she, what-
ever she could carry
of her belongings.
They planned to trav-
el all night so as to
get as far away as
possible by daybreak.
The scheme was well
thought out.  He was to wrap the horses' hooves
and the buggy wheels with grain sacks to obscure
their tracks.  They had hidden food and other

52

provisions in an iron box there in Stoney
Hollow.  They knew that if they could hide
during the days and travel at night, they
could be a hundred miles away in a short
time.

Lucinda could hardly
get through that
last day.  Her
need to pretend
that it was just
another day was
almost more than
she could handle.
That night she
left her home and
family for what
she thought would
be forever.  Tak-
ing that now famil-
iar path over the
hills, she arrived
at their rendezvous
and waited for her
lover to appear.
She waited in vain
most of the night
for the sound of
that horse and
buggy.

Sick with worry and
fear, Lucinda return-
ed home and crept back
into her bedroom.

It was the following day that the community
was alive with the news that the ne'er-do-
well had run off with a yellow-haired girl
from over by the river.

Lucinda's feet carried her rapidly to the secret spot. Her tired and tear-swollen eyes closed forever as she plunged to her death from one of those limestone bluffs.

For years afterwards the ghost of a beautiful young girl could be seen on hot summer nights running along the hill tops in Sherfey's Glen. That ghost eventually took up residence in the vacant home of her ne'er-do-well lover.

Through the years, passers-by would often see small moving lights in that old house and hear the sounds of a weeping girl. On each anniversary of that fateful night long before, the figure of a running girl would be seen along the crest of those hills. On those nights the small blue lights in the house would not appear.

Today there is no one alive who remembers the site of that little house in Sherfey's Glen, and few who even know the area by that name. The passions of those young lovers of over a hundred years ago are long since cooled and only the hills remain.

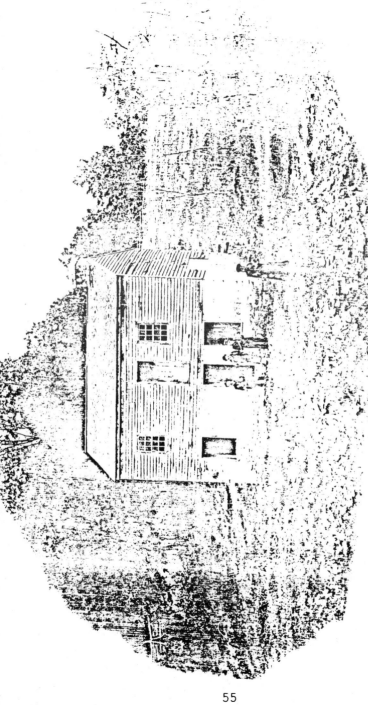

This view shows the home of Lucinda's ne'er-do-well lover as it appeared in 1893.

# CHAPTER X

## THE GHOST OF
## HIWAY #34

e are accustomed to the idea of
haunted houses.  There are also,
of course, haunted cemeteries.
Ghosts have taken up residence
in barns, covered bridges and
even trains.

Burlington is unique in that it has a haunted highway.

The story of the ghost of Highway #34 goes
back to the 1860's when a slave escaped from
a plantation down south.  Like many other
fugitives, he was helped on his way to the
north by abolishionists who hid him in their
houses and barns.  He found his way to a home
on the underground railway in Burlington.
The house was one of those razed to make way
for the new Highway #34 through town.

Plans were being made for this man to stay
here in Iowa.  He was to go on west to a 40
acre farm in the central part of the state.

This farm was being purchased for him by
friends and with money he brought with him
from down south.  He stayed longer in Burlington than was usual while all the arrangements were being made.

While hiding in that house he contracted a
case of diptheria.  Unfortunately, medical
care was necessarily less than ideal under
those secretive conditions.  His health stead-
ily worsened and he finally died in the basement of that house near downtown Burlington.

The records are spotty regarding the details
of his burial, but it is generally understood
that he was buried there in that basement
where he had hidden so long.

This unfortunate man's burial wasn't the end
of him, however.  Now, a century later, he has
been seen on several occasions carrying a
leather bag and trudging along on the north
side of the highway, heading on west.  The
sightings are always between one and two in
the morning.

The most definitive sighting was that when a
motorist picked him up.  As is normal under
those circumstances, the man asked his rider

where he was going and why
at such a late hour of the
night.  His passenger told
him he was heading west to
claim a 40-acre farm that
death had cheated him out
of.  To cover the discom-
fort that answer caused him,
the driver fumbled for a
cigarette.  He lit it, and then glanced once
more over at his strange passenger.  The man

was gone and the car had been going over
sixty miles an hour!  This shaken driver
slammed the car to a stop and searched the
back seat.  Neither the black man nor his
leather bag were to be found.  Quickly, he
turned the car around and drove back a mile
or so, searching the sides of the road, but
to no avail.

Apparently, wherever his friend went, it
wasn't on to his farm because the ghostly
figure of a black man has since been seen
carrying a leather bag, and walking west
along Highway #34.

# CHAPTER XI

## THE WHEEL

It was somewhere in Burlington. The two accounts of the incident that are available differ as to the exact location. Neither of the sources were at all confident of where they thought it to be, so I guess we'll never know.

Wherever it was, this story has to do with a young man who was assumed, by many, to have been the culprit who stole a wheel from a farm wagon. The wagon was parked near a field at the edge of town. Someone sure stole that wheel. The wagon had been jacked up and the wheel was gone. This was of no small matter. A heavy wheel of that nature was of considerable value, and the farmer was faced with the need to purchase another.

This particular young man had not yet been arrested. He had been in a similar scrape before and other circumstances pointed to the distinct possibility of his having committed the deed. The neighbors felt, and apparently he felt, that it was just a matter of time before he would be formally charged with the

crime. He was living with his parents and reportedly had been subjected to a considerable amount of harassment by some.

It was obvious to his parents that their son was distraught by the incident and had been bothered a lot by the allegations made about him.

Perhaps that was the reason he chose to end it all. He arose very early one morning and hung himself from the branch of a large oak tree in their back-yard.

This tragedy weighed heavily on the lad's family. It was especially hard on them when the wagon wheel was found a couple of days later in the hands of another. That person, in fact, confessed to having taken it. That life was wasted over something as trivial as a wagon wheel.

The owner of the wagon had his wheel back. The guilty party received a necessarily light punishment, but the parents of that young man were left with the loss of their son. The boy's father could hardly bring himself to go out into the back-yard. That

large branch overhung the sidewalk.  He
couldn't walk under it but what the grief
of his loss would follow him.  The mother
tried to get her husband to cut the branch
off, but he couldn't bring himself to do
even that.  As things went from bad to worse,
the woman asked a neighbor to come and remove
that cursed limb.  That he did.  It seemed to
help.  Things were getting better after that
until the scar remaining on the tree cracked,
and did so in an odd way.  The cracks were of
a circular pattern;  an almost exact duplica-
tion of the rim and spokes of a wagon wheel.
It was the mother who noticed it first.  She
was dismayed at what she saw.  A circular
design in such weather checking is not uncommon.  What was uncommon about that particular
one was how it duplicated a wagon wheel so
precisely.

This bothered her a lot, but she didn't mention it to her husband for fear that it would
cause him even more grief.  She hoped he
wouldn't see it.  That was too much to hope
for.  He saw it and, as she feared, became
very agitated over that.
They immediately had the
neighbor come back and
completely cut the tree
down.  That was the end
of the tree, but not
the problem.  Very
shortly the same thing
happened to the top of
the stump.  A distinct
pattern of a wagon wheel
appeared.

When the mother saw that, she didn't even
discuss it with her husband.  She hired two
men to come and remove the stump.  That they

did. She even had them fill the hole with black dirt and put sod over the area. When they were done, one would not have even known a tree had stood there.

Apparently, there was to be no rest for this unfortunate couple, for the following year there appeared in the grass, where that tree had been, a perfectly formed fairy ring.

By way of explanation, a fairy ring is a ring of darker and more luxurious grass in a lawn or pasture. These rings can vary from a couple  of feet in diameter to thirty or forty feet. They are formed by a disturbance in the growth pattern of the grass, which is caused, in turn, by an ever widening concentration of a fungus beneath the sod. For some reason the fungus has this effect on the grass. The visual effect is the above-mentioned ring of luxurious grass against a background of shorter and paler green.

This particular fairy ring was an extremely well defined one, about the size of a wagon wheel and stood out very clearly from the rest of the lawn. There was one peculiar difference between this one and others. It had, in addition to the ring, a set of radiating spokes going from the center out to the rim.

This was too much. The couple moved from the house and sold it.

The neighbors watched that area for several years thereafter. The ring came back the following summer. After that the new owner put that portion of yard in garden. The ring was never seen again.

# CHAPTER XII

## THE PICKED CARROTS

ndrew and Sylvia Neuman lived outside of Danville during World War I. Their son, Jason, told this story as he learned it from his mother. Jason was too young in 1913 to understand what was going on. All he remembered is that his father had died. Sylvia told him later the bizarre events that followed Andrew's death.

Like all couples, Andrew and Sylvia had minor areas of disagreement. Most of these were insignificant and little attention was paid to them. One of these had been long in brewing and dealt with the garden. It was "When to pick the carrots?"

Andrew always insisted on picking them while they were yet very small "cause they were good and tasty then."

"Besides, I want those tender tops to feed the ducks," he would explain.

Sylvia would have preferred to let them mature. She felt they got but little return for their effort in those tiny little carrots.

Andrew, however, had his way on the issue. First of all, it was he who raised them. Secondly, once a carrot is pulled, it's pulled. Andrew would pull them up when he felt it was time to do so, and that was the end of the argument for yet another year.

It was while gardening one day when Andrew died. He had been pushing one of those garden plows when he suddenly stopped, sat down in a row, and died.

Andrew had always been the main-stay there in the garden, but Sylvia picked up that responsibility the following year. She gardened some-what differently than he in several respects. One of these was her re-solve to let those carrots go until mature.

This anticipation was small consolation for her having lost her husband. When the carrots matured to the point at which Andrew would have picked them, it was a sad day for Sylvia. She would have preferred to have her annual "carrot argument," but those days were gone.

It was at this point that Andrew's will first began to show itself. One morning Sylvia went to the garden and found over half a row of those tender young carrots pulled and lying neatly in a row. This was a chilling sight for her. They were in that row exactly as Andrew had placed them when he was alive. Sylvia could find no one who would confess to having done that.

The next morning found the rest of that row picked and part of a second one. This was too much! That night Sylvia and a neighbor lady sat on the porch and watched. It was a still and moonlit night and those remaining rows of carrots were easy to see from the screened-in porch.

Sylvia felt a bit foolish asking her neighbor to stand watch with her, but she was determined to find out who or what was pulling her carrots. She felt the neighbor was just humoring her by sitting up with her that night.

It was about 1:00 A.M., and Sylvia was talking to her friend about some totally different matter. She saw the woman suddenly lean forward and stare wide-eyed at the garden. Sylvia turned in time to see two rows of those

carrot tops wildly waving back and forth. Both
women were totally shocked. Each carrot top
was jerking violently in a whipping action.
The other plants were standing quite still on
that night when there was no wind.

The neighbor lady jumped to her feet and fled
to the interior of the house. Sylvia's fascin-
ation with what was happening in the garden
took a temporary back seat as she rushed in to
comfort her friend. She found her in the kitchen.

"You stay here, and I'll be right back," she
shouted and returned to the porch within but a
few seconds.

The wild waving of the tops had stopped. The
rows were picked clean, and there in the moon-
light were two long and neat lines of carrots,
young and tender. They were lain just as
Andrew had always done.

# CHAPTER XIII

## MARJORIE

The doll was originally a quite ordinary one. That is, it wasn't particularly fancy or expensive or from some exotic place. In fact, it was common enough that no one in the family remembered where it came from.

Even though the doll's ownership wasn't firmly established, Becky Soule claimed it. However, her little sister, Ann, played with

it more than Becky did. That toy was one of
several dolls and stuffed animals that Ann
pushed around in her baby buggy. Like little
dolls and little girls everywhere, Dollie was
simply part of the children's play time.

Becky and Ann lived with their parents in a
large and old stone house between Burlington
and Mediapolis. It was on some of that rough
ground just off Hiway #99.

The only thing the Soules knew about any previous residents, they learned from the edge of
the kitchen door where some pencil lines and
notes charted the growth of a Marjorie and an
Alfred. The marks stopped soon under Marjorie's
name, leading the Soules to assume that she had
died at an early age. They left those crude
records out of deference to those otherwise un-
known earlier residents. Besides there was

something intriguing about the abrupt end of
Marjorie's growth record. The Soules made no
association, at first, between the long ago
Marjorie and the doll that Ann played with.

The incident that made the Soule family realize they had a ghost in their home was in the
fall of 1926. They left the house for a few
hours on a short trip. As they got into the
car, Mrs. Soule found two or three dolls in
the front seat. She gathered them up and
pitched them onto the sofa through the front
door and got back into the car. Among those
was Dollie, the non-descript one that was
destined to become the object of great curiosity and even of fear.

When the family returned, Mrs. Soule was surprised to find the dolls there on the sofa
except for Dollie. She was in the next room,
sitting on the floor by a box of blocks.
Eight of the blocks were neatly arranged,
spelling MARJORIE. Mrs. Soule was simply
unable to figure out how that one doll had
gotten into the next room. Her daughters
were with her on that trip, and the house
was empty. Further, she was really concerned
about those blocks. Who set them out to spell
MARJORIE? Did that have anything to do with
the Marjorie recorded there on the edge of
the door into the kitchen?

The block incident and the resulting conversation about it there in the fam-
ily caused the girls to recall
some other strange things about
that doll.

Ann remembered one time when
Dollie had different clothes on

71

in the morning than she had the night before.

"Don't you remember me telling you about that?" Ann asked her mother.

Mrs. Soule didn't, but she knew she would have dismissed it without giving it much thought anyway.

At this point, Becky chimed in.

"Another thing;  I told you about the time Dollie had tear stains on her cheeks after Ann spanked her for being bad one day.  Also, she had a bracelet on the other arm than I had put it on."

The realization, by the family, that Dollie was not an ordinary toy made them view her in an altogether different light.  First of all, Ann changed Dollie's name to Marjorie.  She felt that if little Marjorie of years earlier had somehow taken up residence in the body of that doll, they could at least call her by her right name.

This strange situation of the apparent occupation of a doll's body by the ghost of a child wasn't something the family was able to forget. Additional things followed.

On one occasion, Mr. Soule was playing with their pet dog on the living room floor.  He was having the dog do tricks for him.  Mr. Soule was unaware of "Marjorie" being there in the room until he heard a distinct cry of delight coming from over by the wall just as the dog was doing a particularly good trick.  Looking over there, he saw Marjorie propped up against the baseboard with her head turned in the direction of the dog.

Mr. Soule sat there for quite awhile looking at that doll. The only occupants of the house were he and the dog. Yet, he knew that little exclamation had been real.

It was with more than just a little hesitation that he went over and picked up that toy. As usual, she appeared to be a normal and ordinary doll. He stuck the doll into the toy box. He

wasn't very comfortable having a haunted doll for an audience.

It was after the dog incident that Mr. and Mrs. Soule decided to get rid of the doll once and for all.

Needless to say, they were at a bit of a loss
as to how to do it. They couldn't bring themselves to bury or burn it since that doll act-
ed as if it were alive.

Before they could come up with a solution to
their problem, another thing happened. Ann
found a long and sharp needle in Marjorie's
hand. It was tightly clutched between those
little wooden fingers. Both girls were very
afraid and both firmly denied putting that
needle in Marjorie's hand.

That needle incident was just too much! Mr.
and Mrs. Soule vowed to get rid of that crea-
ture one way or the other that day. A neighbor's auction that very afternoon provided the
opportunity. Mrs. Soule went to the auction,
slipped Marjorie into a box of toys, and returned home. She didn't know who, if anyone,
bought that box of toys. She did know that
their family was rid of that doll with the
ghost of a little girl.

The Soules continued to live in that old stone
house for many years and never again heard or
saw anything out of the ordinary among their
children's toys.

## CHAPTER XIV

## PEGLEG NELSON

ustov Nelson had but one leg when
he moved into the community east
of Augusta back sometime after the
Civil War. The only known records
of Gustov are some found in the
neighbor's family scrapbook. These records
don't explain how he lost his leg. It was
assumed, however, that he was a
Civil War vet and lost it in
that great conflict.

Gustov's claim to fame (beyond
his considerable ability to
negotiate on one good leg and
one wooden one) was his un-
rivaled ability to consume
great quantities of whiskey.
He credited that to the fact
that he had a hollow leg.

Gustov was not shy about his
wooden leg nor did he dwell
on it. He wore it all the
time, but didn't bother to
take care of it. That leg

went quite shoeless.

As the years passed, Gustov's body showed the ravages of what was probably some of the worst rotgut in Des Moines County. He grew old rapidly; blaming the weather, hard work, mean horses, just about everything to hard winters other than the voluminous quantities of that whiskey he drank. His wooden leg fared no better. That unshod appendage had stomped uncounted miles through mud, ice, snow, slush, and dust. It was weatherbeaten and cracked. A friend had taken the opportunity to carve his initials on it one night as Gustov laid on his bed drunk. A mare of approximately the same intelligence had clumsily stepped on that foot, cracking a good-sized chip from it. All in all, Gustov and his foot looked pretty much alike.

Old Gustov could sure enough drink like no
other man around. He could also sing like
none other. The problem was that it was a
whole lot worse than others, not better.
Many nights he could be heard bellowing his
way down the dirt road from Augusta to his
shack in the woods
where he did a
little half-
hearted farm-
ing and some
hunting for
a living.
Usually,
when they
could be
understood,
his songs
dealt with
times long
ago, places
far away,
and loves
long cooled.
What his vo-
cal bombasts
lacked in
quality, they

made up for in volume. More than one mother
would tuck her children in bed at night saying,
"Listen out there, that's what whiskey and bad
companions will do to you."

There finally comes an end to all things, even
bad neighbors and awful songs. Eventually, it
came time to commit Gustov to his final resting
place. The "service" was out in the woods and
was attended by a few seedy-looking characters
representing various, if almost indiscernible,
degrees of sobriety. The affair was led by a
friend qualified to do that sort of thing.

His qualifications consisted of his having both an uncle and a brother who had attended missionary school. The uncle had, in fact, lasted at that school for almost a year.

The local authorities allowed the "funeral" to take place out under that big oak tree on the theory that the participants were better doing that than being somewhere else getting into more serious trouble. Besides, there was a general air of relief within the community. It was finally rid of one of that ragtag bunch of ne'er-do-wells.

That's where they were wrong. Shortly after the funeral, a local farmer and his wife were returning home from Burlington one night and came upon a peg-legged drunk walking down the road. Having just come from church and being dressed up and all, they didn't bother to stop to offer a ride or other help. Only later did they realize that the man they had seen was none other than Gustov!

A few months later, a salesman driving to Mt. Pleasant did give a lift to a man with a wooden leg. When the salesman described the incident later at an inn in Mt. Pleasant, others asked for details. As he spun his story, it became obvious that he had picked up old Gustov.

The last evidence of Gustov being seen was the following January. There had been a January thaw and the roadways were soft. One night the unmistakable roar of Gustov's drinking songs were heard along the River Road that went east out of Augusta. Three different farmers, all of a sober and serious nature, heard Gustov that night.

By sunup, the surface of that elongated mud strip that pretended to be a road was frozen hard. Cast in that mud were alternating prints of a man's shoe and a weather-beaten stump of a wooden leg. The tracks wove a slightly wobbly path along the side of that road that had been so often traveled by Gustov Nelson in life.

# CHAPTER XV

## JONAS

Jonas was a hired man for James Welke who lived between Oakville and Mediapolis in the 1920's.

The relationship between Jonas and the Welkes was not a good one from the very beginning. Jonas did not come well recommended and the Welkes didn't need a man all that badly anyway. It was something of an accommodation on their part to hire him. It was one of those situations in which the man needed to be taken in and the Welkes knew that if they didn't, no one would.

Jonas was apparently of a contrary and quarrelsome nature. This caused an early and permanent erosion in their relationship. For a hired man, he had an uncommonly long list of farm chores he simply wouldn't do. Unfortunately, for James, that list included just about every chore that was distasteful, difficult, or uncomfortable. Mr. Welke had to work around that situation and either do those jobs himself or see them go undone.

One of these jobs that Jonas wouldn't do was
to sweep the hundreds of pounds of alfalfa
leaves left on the floor of the hayloft when
the hay was all gone.  Mr. Welke liked to get
those cleaned out each spring.  The roof of
the barn was not the best and
that mixture of fine dust and
leaf fragments would get wet
in some spots.  He wanted
that out of there so the
moisture wouldn't rot out
his floor.  It seemed that
there was never a good time
for that distasteful chore.
When it was dry, it would
cake on in spots and also raise large clouds of
dust that would permeate a man's clothes.  When
it was wet, it would be heavy, and hard to work

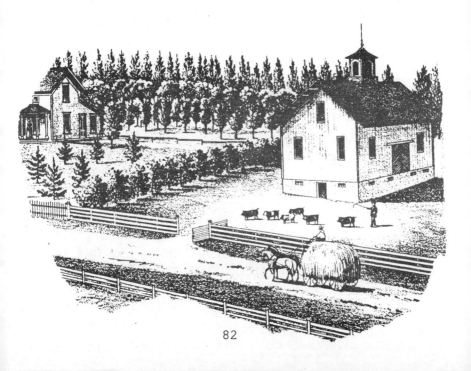

82

with. It wasn't an overwhelming problem,
but it was a job that Jonas just didn't
want any part of.

The first year that Jonas worked for the
Welkes, James ended up doing that loft job
himself. The second year, he was less in-
clined to be so accommodating. He insisted
that Jonas do it. After a good deal of ar-
guing back and forth, Jonas finally accepted
the inescapable. The job was done both reluctantly and poorly. More to make a point
than anything else, Mr. Welke insisted that
it be done, redone, and done again until it
was clean to his satisfaction. James was
totally exasperated by the time it was over
and Jonas was hoppin' mad.

The two men argued about that issue most of
the evening, as well as for several days
thereafter. Even their chess game for which
they had usually declared a nightly truce
was left unplayed for those several days.
The situation went from
bad to worse. Jonas
widened the argument
to making some pretty
pointed observations
about James's manage-
ment abilities. Mr.
Welke, in turn, found
it a good time to com-
plain about a long list
of problems he had with
Jonas. Things got pretty
hot. Mr. Welke was about ready to send Jonas
packing down the road. He was tired of the
whole situation.

Jonas had a talent for doing everything at the
wrong time. This time was no exception. He

got himself kicked in the neck by one of the donkeys. He apparently also suffered a serious head injury because he fell into a coma.

The days-long argument was forgotten. All the right things were done. A doctor was summoned and Jonas was given the best possible care.

Old Jonas lost his quarrel with the Grim Reaper and died within a few days.

While Jonas was buried in a Potter's Field with little in terms of unnecessary expenses, it was a decent funeral and he was buried with dignity. Mr. Welke even had the decency to get rid of the donkey that had kicked old Jonas, almost giving it away in order to get rid of it.

The following day James was in the barn and looked ruefully at that big pile of hay dust on the floor where it had fallen when swept out of the loft. He felt badly about having participated in that argument. The whole thing seemed awfully petty now that old Jonas was dead and buried. He resolved to get rid of that the next day.

That night the dog did a lot of barking and carrying on. He was supposed to, of course. That is what watchdogs are for. This particular dog was always more eager to bark than he was discriminating, so James didn't give it much thought when he had to holler at that mutt several times to be quiet. He thought it was simply another

one of his spells of making
a lot of noise for no reason.

Morning brought the recol-
lection that Mr. Welke had
promised himself to get rid
of that pile of haydust.
He decided to do that the first thing and get
that unpleasant issue behind him.

Entering the barn, Mr. Welke was surprised to
find that pile of haydust gone.  All that remained was a bit scattered around.  He then
noticed that the back door of the barn was
open and surmised that his cows had been in
there and had eaten
some of that stuff
and scattered the
rest of it.

That was the end of
that incident, ex-
cept for a few days
of worry lest these
cows had gotten too
much of that fine
dust and would take
sick.  They didn't,
so life continued
on as normal.

That is, it was normal for awhile.  Mr. Welke
had no occasion to go back up into that loft
until early summer when he climbed up there
in preparation for putting new hay in it.

There on the floor of the loft was that haydust that he thought the cows had eaten earlier.
It was all there, well spread out, just about
how it was when Jonas had to clean it up.

85

James stood looking at that floor and was
thinking of how his dog had barked so much
the night after they buried Jonas.  He re-
called that the dog had been running back
and forth between the house and the barn.
As he surveyed that loft floor, he was glad
he didn't go out to investigate what the dog
was barking about that night.

James Welke went back to the house to tell his
wife that old Jonas won that argument they had
the week before he died.

# CHAPTER XVI

## THE OLD BRICK INN

It was an old house just off Agency Road when it served as an inn. It wasn't an official stop for the stage, but passengers could be dropped off there. If there was room on the stage the next day, they could be picked up again. If there wasn't room, the stranded travelers were stuck for another full day.

Most people wouldn't stay at that inn for fear of not being able to leave again the following day. Some, however, would put up with that risk just for the opportunity to spend an evening at The Old Brick Inn. The "Brick's" beds weren't the softest. They, in fact, harbored their own quota of livestock in the form of assorted bugs, mice, lice, and whatever. The food was tolerable, no better and no worse than that found in countless other inns in the Midwest. Since the Old Brick Inn wasn't an official stop, its management wasn't responsible to any stage line's standards. As a result, it was rather loosely run.

The "Brick's" main attraction (in fact, its only real attraction) was the frequency, duration, and nature of its parties. Most inns advertised themselves as being havens of peace and quiet for the road weary traveler. The rigors of travel by stage or horseback made such quiet and restful places a welcome sight for most people. Not so with The Brick. Any

traveler who arrived less than eager to drink, dance, sing, and pinch bottoms was in for a disappointment. Few nights passed without a rip-roaring party at The Brick.

Unsuspecting guests who expected a few hours of rest and relaxation were, on occasion, seen going down the road in the middle of the night to escape the noise. There were generally those who had had the foresight to arrive by horseback rather than on the stage.

These parties were the idea and the delight of the proprietor of "The Brick." John O'Neal was an Irishman of endless energy and capacity for food, fun, and frolic.

John and his family lived there at the Inn. The family consisted of him, his wife, and several grandchildren who had been orphaned at early ages. Each member of the family learned, through long experience, to tolerate the endless parties there at The Old Brick Inn.

John's grandson, Peter, was one of those children and spent his youth there at the inn. This story was told by Peter's daughter many years later.

Like the others in the family, Peter had responsibilities for some of the many chores associated with operating an inn. Peter's chores, among others, consisted of tending the rather large flock of chickens, geese, and guineas the O'Neals raised for the kitchen.

Peter stayed on in the Burlington area long after the eventual death of his grandparents and the scattering of his brothers and sisters. The inn was vacated, then neglected. It fell into disrepair, soon becoming a mere brick shell of the busy and dynamic place it had been. Within a few years, it was torn down in order to farm the site. The next summer

a field of oats waved where earlier dancers
had kept pace with the music that was gone.
The music was replaced by the silence of a
farmer's field.

Peter thought often of his childhood there in the inn.  He thought of his strong-willed and fun-loving grandfather.  He remembered of how he with his brothers and sisters would "make do" with whatever toys they could devise.

He thought of his grandmother's many bird-houses and how she would save the scraps from the table for her feathered "children."

But, the days of youthful games were gone. The
nights of parties were over. Peter was quite
sure of that until one night when he met a
traveler in a bar in Lowell. The two men sat
trading conversation. The traveler told of his
stumbling onto a real neat place not too far
from where they sat there in Lowell.

"This place was all done up in antiques and was
in the decor of an old-fashioned country inn."

Peter only half listened. It was simply another story about another cutesy night spot,
and he was past being interested in that sort
of thing. The traveler went on to describe the
place he'd spent the previous night. He told
about how it was done up and how he really had
a good time there at a party.

Peter began to wonder just where this place was
that the stranger was so enthused about. He'd
been in that part of Des Moines County for many
years and couldn't place it. Besides that, it
was kind of intriguing how that nightspot sound-
ed so much like The Old Brick Inn of his youth.

The stranger couldn't be real specific about
exactly where the place was, but described its
location well enough that Peter realized that
no such nightspot was anywhere near there.

This intrigued Peter no end. How could this be?
Where had the stranger been? He asked more questions. The man was really warmed up to the subject by now and described the place in detail.

Slowly at first, then in a rush of confusion and
dismay, Peter realized the traveler was describing The Old Brick Inn. The man told about the
rooms and old John O'Neal perfectly. Additional
questions simply added to the mystery. The man

had spent the evening before at Peter's home
of years ago!

It took all the self-control Peter could mus-
ter to stay calm and to casually suggest that
the two of them go to that inn for a drink.
The stranger agreed and offered to drive.

Peter's daughter told of how her father remembered having to fight back tears, excitement and panic as they drove the few miles
to the place.  In a short while, the man got
his bearings and announced that "he knew how
to get there from here."

The small talk and the darkness hid Peter's
growing excitement as they approached the
site of his boyhood home.

"It's just over the rise here.  I'm surprised
you didn't know about this place."

Peter could only nod, his throat drawn tight
and his mouth was dry.  He didn't need to be
told what was just over the rise.  It was on
this very
spot in the
road where
he had kil-
led a small
bird with a
slingshot.
He had gone
down this
hill many
times on a
sled.

As the car
came over
the rise,

the stranger prepared to pull off into the
parking lot he had used the night before.
His headlights revealed no parking lot and
no nightclub "all done up in antiques." There
was only a farmer's access to a cornfield.

The stranger was struck dumb. After he gathered his wits the best he could, he said: "I
know this is the place. This has to be the
place. Where is it?"

Peter didn't answer. He simply got out and
stood there looking down those straight corn
rows. Thoughts raced through his head.

"How could it be?

"Was his new friend
really there just
the previous night?

"Was his grandfa-
ther there, having
one of his endless
parties?

"Was he there, him-
self, last night as
a child?

"Were his brothers
and sisters there?

"How about the lit-
tle girl from whom
he had stolen his
first kiss?"

Peter's daughter
went on to tell of
how her father told

of standing in the chill of the night. Of
how he thought about his boyhood, his grandfather, and The Old Brick Inn.

She told of how he had said: "I guess at
some point the stranger left. When I finally gathered my wits about me, he was
gone. All I could see were his tire tracks
from where we pulled into that access. He
probably wondered what was wrong with me,
and just took off."

## CHAPTER XVII

## THE ARM

eil and Lee Simmons were brothers who lived between Sperry and Kingston. Apparently, neither were married as they lived together in a cabin down along the creek.

The records don't tell us what these two men did for a living, when they lived, or exactly where.

This story comes from a lady in Burlington whose grandfather knew these men and had written an account of the events that led to their inclusion in this book.

The brothers had entered into a short-term contract for which they were to cut some timbers for planking to be used in a railroad bridge. For these, they were clearing some large timber out on Huron Island.

That was long before the days of chain saws. The Simmons used one of those long two-man cross-cut saws. These were six to eight feet long with vertical handles on each end.

As one man pulled, the other simply held onto
his handle to keep the saw from whipping back
and forth.  He also bore down slightly to help
the teeth grab the wood.  A half second or so
later, they reversed their roles and the other
then held on to prevent the saw from whipping.
This procedure was followed until the entire
cut was made.  When the saw was sharp and had
a good stout man on each end, a cross-cut could
go through a log in a hurry.

The brothers had worked long and hard out there
on Huron Island one warm fall day.  The work
was strenuous, and Neil had taken his shirt off.
The tattoo of a sailing ship on his arm bobbed
about as his muscles worked back and forth.  It
was almost as if the ship was on a heavy sea,
being tossed by waves.

Suddenly, the chain holding the nearby wagon-
load of logs snapped.  Those huge logs came
rolling out like so many tinker toys.  Neil
jumped aside, but too late.  His arm was
crushed between two massive hickories.

Lee rushed his brother to a neighbor from where
a doctor was summoned.  He was then taken to

Burlington and the mangled arm was removed.

The timber on Huron Island was neglected the next few days as Neil made a temporary recovery. The two men planned to continue their lives here in Des Moines County and had even started to work out how they would do things, what with Neil lacking one arm. They knew that there would have to be changes.

The changes in store were much more profound than either realized. Neil contracted a severe infection. He went into a coma from which he never recovered. He died within a few days.

The lady's account of this story leaves some gaps and goes directly to Lee returning to Huron Island to work again in the timber; this time, by himself.

The two-man saw had but one man to operate it now. This is possible through a little trick that woodsmen have practiced for many years. A single operator can prevent the whipping of the other end by putting his hat on that far handle. The weight of the hat is usually enough to prevent the whipping action. Lee did that and got along just fine. It was a bit slower and more laborious, but it worked.

A few days after Neil's death, Lee was running that old cross-cut, using his hat as a partner. That can be mindless work. As he pulled and

pushed on the saw, he had his eyes on the ground and was lost in thought. His body was working hard, but his thoughts were off somewhere else.

Suddenly, his load lightened. The saw was going through the log quicker and it felt as if someone was pulling on his "push" stroke. Confused, Lee peered up over the log to see what was going on.

His hat was no longer on that other handle. It was lying on the ground. In its place was a dismembered arm, its muscles glistening with the sweat on that hot day. On the upper part of the arm was a tattoo of a ship. That ship was bobbing back and forth as if buffeted by the waves of a high sea.

With a scream of terror, Lee let go of the saw. As he did so, the other end dropped down behind the log. Hardly able to make his arms and legs obey his will, he climbed up over the log. There he saw only the other end of the cross-cut and his hat lying on the ground.

Did Lee daydream himself into a vision? Or was that arm really there?

We don't know. All we know is that Lee left the saw. He left a pile of logs there and a contract unfilled. Lee disappeared from the community and never was heard of again.

## CHAPTER XVIII

## THE ARGUMENT

illian Hawkins was a quite proper spinster of mature age. She lived with her elderly mother on a small farm between Dodgeville and Highway #99, approximately just before the turn of the century.

Small as their place was, they did nothing toward farming it. The few acres of tillable ground were rented out and the pasture was also rented to a neighbor. Lillian and her mother lived on a soldier's pension earned by Mr. Hawkins. Her grand niece in Danville who told this story assumed that there was also a small inheritance from which the ladies drew against as the need arose.

The two ladies busied themselves with running the house, carrying on a correspondence with relatives and doing some of what today would be called "crafts." Like many who engage in that sort of thing now, they enjoyed making decorative items for wall hangings. These were used in their own home and some were sent to friends and relatives.

This story that deals with the Hawkins' ladies revolves around one of those craft projects.

Their favorite craft was what they called "pebble pretties." Apparently, a pebble pretty was a slab formed by gluing small colorful pebbles together on a table. This slab would be allowed to dry, a wire attached, then hung on the wall. Pebbles of a color, size, and shape would be selected so that when all were arranged, the result would be a recognizable pattern. The pebbles would all be held together with generous quantities of wallpaper paste. The final product would be one to three feet in diameter and an inch or so thick. The larger the piece and the smaller the rocks, the more details could be worked into the final product.

The good ladies would spend countless hours down at the creek collecting pebbles and even more time putting them all together. They worked these things most evenings. Needless to say, these jigsaw puzzle-like things took a lot of time and energy.

Lillian and her mother tended to each work on her own "pebble pretty" rather than to do one together. This was mainly because they would invariably get into an argument about what pattern to make, what rocks to use, etc. These arguments would get quite heated, so they had learned to avoid them by each having her own project to work on.

This was a sensible approach. Unfortunately, they decided against their instincts one day and chose to do one together. This was to be a special one. They wanted to give one to Lillian's sister in Danville. She and her husband were to be soon celebrating their twenty-fifth wedding anniversary. That decision to do a "pebble pretty" together was a poor one. Things were destined to go downhill from that point on.

Mrs. Hawkins thought a picture of the couple would be nice. She suggested that the sandstone rocks down by the creek would be just  right for the skin tones for her son-in-law's face and the lighter colored chert would do for the lighter face of her daughter.

Lillian thought that such a portrait would be too traditional and tame. She wanted to do a picture of a wild horse standing on a windswept hill. Her sister and brother-in-law raised horses, so she felt that would be just the thing.

This trivial difference of opinion soon degenerated into a full-fledged argument. Lillian held out for the horse and her mother for the portrait of the couple.

The two ladies couldn't agree. They did start the outside edge with a neutral color suitable for either subject, but still hadn't resolved the key issue. As the project progressed, there came a point where they had to go one way or the other. It was then that the argument changed into a real crisis with bad feelings on both sides.

Finally, Mrs. Hawkins announced that she was washing her hands of the whole thing and

that, as far as she was concerned, Lillian
could do whatever she wanted.

Lillian did just that.  The fun was out of it
by now, but she was determined to finish the
piece anyway.  Evening after evening Lillian
worked on that "pebble pretty."  Each stone
was carefully selected;  each was turned over
and over as she searched for the right color
and shape to form that image of a horse.  She
used sand to form the delicate hairs of the
mane and tail.  These looked as if the wind
was whipping them around.  Tiny pieces of
mother-of-pearl were used to make the ani-
mal's hooves.

Lillian was doing a fine job
on the "pebble pretty."  If
her mother admired the work,
she said nothing.  That long
argument and its daily re-
minder on the table grated
on her nerves.  The poi-
soned environment took its
toll on the relationship
between the two ladies, and
hostility was the order of
the day.  Both knew the
whole affair was silly, but
both were too stubborn to
let it go.

Finally, after many weeks, the piece was done.
The newspaper on which the project lay had
even turned a little yellow.

It was at this point that Mrs. Hawkins took
very sick.  She was very old and Lillian's
concern was well-founded.

Even as her mother lie on her deathbed, this

proper concern of Lillian's was met with
anger and resentment. The end approached
and she was slipping fast.

Lillian chose that time to try to make amends
and she told her mother then that she was
sorry about their long and pointless argument. Mrs. Hawkins' response was simply:
"You will see, I'll have my way."

Lillian not only lost her mother, but she
also found it necessary to get the house all
spruced up for the funeral. That next day,
a friend helped her turn the now cured "pebble pretty" over so she could soak the newspaper off the back.

There on the back of the "pebble pretty" was
the most shocking thing Lillian had ever seen.
In place of the normal and nondescript array
of pebbles forming a random mix of colors and
shapes was a distinct pattern. It was, of
course, formed by the backsides of the pebbles used to form the image of the horse on
front. The picture was a faithful reproduc-
tion of the appearance of the couple about
to celebrate their anniversary. The labori-
ously placed sand that made the horse's mane
and tail also formed her sister's "hair" and
the couch upon which her brother-in-law sat.
The back sides of those little pieces of
mother-of-pearl served as buttons on the man's
coat.

Lillian's mind raced back to her mother's
words spoken on her deathbed:

"You will see, I'll have my way."

# CHAPTER XIX

## THE PRIZE QUILT

Mrs. Harold Knil of Burlington died in 1933.

Her earthly possessions were modest at best. A variety of ill luck had dogged her and the late Mr. Knil for a good part of their married lives, and they had found it impossible to accumulate very much. Among her possessions was, however, one item of considerable value. It was a large and well-made quilt. That quilt was all handmade and was a kaleidoscope of colors and patterns. Mrs. Knil had won top honors with it at the state fair in Texas where they had lived earlier. That prize-winning quilt was of top quality and well cared for.

The quilt was not only of excellent workmanship, but was something special within the family. Mrs. Knil had sewn, with tiny delicate stitches, a symbol of the trade of each of several of the men in the relationship. There were

designs to represent the tools of a sailor, a
doctor, a farmer, weigh-master, a maker of
cheese, and many others.

Mrs. Knil had arranged for the proper division
of her belongings prior to her death.  The quilt
was to go to her son in Cali-
fornia.  Others of her children were promised other
things.

Unfortunately, that quilt,
along with other items, was
in the possession of an ex-
daughter-in-law in Yarmouth.
At the time of the divorce
from Mrs. Knil's son, that
young lady was to have returned these things to
Mrs. Knil.  She didn't, however, so it made for
a rather sticky situation.  It was, in fact, one
of those situations tailor-made for a nasty family argument.  And so it happened.  The son wrote
to his ex-sister-in-law
for the quilt.  She told
him that she had it, but
that she would be keeping
it.

The ensuing barrage of
letters from the son
demanding the quilt
was to no avail.  She
had that beautiful
thing and had no inten-
tion of parting with
it;  especially to
the brother of the man
for whom she had some
pretty bitter feelings.

One night as the errant ex-daughter-in-law and her husband were sitting in the living room listening to the radio, he thought he heard a noise coming from the bedroom. He decided it must have been his imagination as he strained to hear over the static of that early radio. He, therefore, dismissed it without investigating. A minute or so later, they both heard a distinct thump from that bedroom. Even the cat sleeping by the fireplace woke up with a start. The couple went into that room to see what was happening.

Standing by the bed was Mrs. Knil. This was more than a small surprise since she had been dead for almost three months by that time. The couple stared at the lady for a minute before looking at each other in shock. The husband started to say something, but was interrupted by Mrs. Knil raising her arm in an angry manner as if to silence him. Being less than anxious to argue with a ghost, he said nothing.

Then, without a word, that image of Mrs. Knil
faded away and was gone.

It took a minute for the couple to regain their
composure. When they did, they compared what
they had seen. They agreed even down to the
type and color of clothes worn by Mrs. Knil.

They stayed up late that night discussing what
had happened and wondering if they should tell
anyone else. They hesitated to do so for fear
of being ridiculed. They still hadn't decided
what to do about it when they finally went to
bed. It was with some reluctance that they
even decided to sleep at all in their bedroom
after their experience.

The mystery deepened as soon as they got into
the bed. The night was less chilly than those
just preceding it, yet there didn't seem to be
enough covers. The
wife made some feeble
attempts at a joke
about how they had
been so scared that
they were still cold
from it. As she threw

back the covers to fetch another blanket, she
noticed that there did indeed seem to be fewer
covers than there should have been. When she
investigated, she found that something was missing. That quilt that she had under the bed-
spread was gone. It was the same quilt that she

had gotten from Mrs. Knil and
about which she had been having
that long argument with her ex-
brother-in-law. That quilt had
been on the bed for several
weeks; yet now it was gone.
She had, in fact, changed the

bedding just a day or two earlier and knew that she had put the quilt back on the bed just as she had done many times before.

It would be nice to be able to report that the quilt turned up in the home of the son in California that same night. Alas, the story can't be wrapped up quite that neatly. The account of this incident came from a grandson of Mrs. Knil who presently lives in Burlington. When he learned the story from his grandparents, they didn't know if the son ended up with the quilt or not.

So, we are only left to speculate. That quilt with all the pretty colors, patterns, and symbols had to be somewhere, and it sure wasn't on the bed that eventful night in Yarmouth in 1933.

# CHAPTER XX

## GREAT GRANDFATHER LEAMAN

This story comes to us from a long time ago, yet in some detail. For that we can thank the foresight of Emily Leaman. She recognized a dramatic moment when she saw one and had the good sense to have her daughter write it all down. It was from that account written a century ago that the following tale is taken. The original handwritten account rests securely today in a safety deposit box in Burlington.

Ed Leaman, his wife, Emily, and their four children lived west of Oakville on a small farm in the 1880's. Ed ended up on that farm after a lot of moves, both as a child and as a married adult. Others in his family had moved a lot, also. As a result, Ed's knowledge of his family's kin was sketchy. About all he really knew was that they had come from New England and were mostly cabinet makers and fishermen.

This sort of thing wasn't of much interest to Ed anyway. He had plenty enough to think about to provide for his family without worrying over stuff like that. He neither knew, nor cared, about what had happened earlier.

Ed's son, Keith, was an average sort of lad with nothing about him to suggest anything supernatural or otherwise out of the ordinary. However, when the boy was nine, he told his parents one morning that he was lying in bed

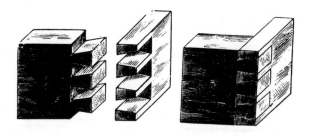

the previous evening, and a man appeared to him. The man explained that he was Ed's grandfather and thought it would be nice to chat awhile with his grandson's son.

Keith said that he and his unexpected visitor spent about an hour talking that evening. The old man told him about life in New England. He told of how he had been an officer in the Colonial Army during the Revolutionary War. The old man, in fact, gave Keith a small purse containing a few buttons, a pipe, and a small brass penknife with his initials, L.T.L., engraved in the handle.

Neither Ed nor Emily could understand why their son insisted on that strange story. They could see the purse of trinkets, of course, but assumed that the boy found it or something. A neighbor diagnosed the problem immediately. He observed:

"Well, what do you expect? If you let a boy waste as much time with book larnin' as that one of yours does, you can expect for him to get some strange ideas."

Keith persisted in his version of what happened. After a period of anger on his parents' part, the incident was eventually forgotten.

The next time the old man appeared, Keith just didn't mention it to his parents. All he got the first time for his trouble was a reprimand for lying or daydreaming.

The old man appeared several more times, always in Keith's bedroom in the evening. They had some good visits; the elder Leaman seemed to enjoy these chats as much as Keith did. Keith was thrilled to learn about all the exciting things his great grandfather and others in

the family had done many years earlier.  He
learned of a shipwreck that the old man and
his brothers had seen and had rowed out to in
a rowboat to save some of the sailors.

This went on for several months.  Sometimes the
visits would last but a few minutes and others
would go on for a couple of hours.  Keith was
too young to understand what could have been
going on, yet old enough to know that whatever
it was, it wasn't normal.  He knew of ghosts,

of course, and figured that his great-grandfather was one of them.  He just accepted the
situation rather than to try to cipher it all
out.

On one of the old man's visits, he told Keith
that it would be the last one and that he would-
n't be seeing him anymore.  And sure enough, it
was indeed the last time the lad chatted with

his great-grandfather.

It was a year or two later that Keith told
his mother of those subsequent conversations
with the old man. Again, his revelation was
met with disbelief and more than a little
anger. She told him that he could not tell
his father about that and it would be best
if he would just forget it.

Several years went by and Keith was 18 or 19
when a letter came to Ed. It was from Ed's
sister, Janet, in Attleboro, Massachusetts.
She told him that her husband had talked her
into doing some investigation into their
"family tree." She went on to explain that
she had done just that and had learned some
things about the family that she and Ed had-
n't known. She told him that she wanted to
tell him and Emily about it and that she could
do so because she and her husband were making
a trip to Chicago. They could, if it was al-
right, come on down to visit.

After a couple of
letters back and
forth, all the
arrangements
were made.
Janet and
her husband
would be coming
to Burlington.
Ed and Emily
would pick them
up there and take
them on to Oak-
ville for a visit.

It had been quite awhile since Ed and Janet had
seen each other so the forthcoming visit caused

a bit of a stir in the family.

Then finally one day, Janet and her husband
came.  There were the regulation number of
mummers about "It's certainly been a long
time," or "My, how you've grown."  Relatives
were something of an oddity in the Leaman home
so the whole affair was pretty exciting.

After supper that first night, Janet unpacked
a bundle of papers, certificates, letters, and
so forth.  She had collected these in her "Family tree" work and went over them with Ed and
Emily.  The children showed interests varying
from none to great, depending on how exciting
was the issue being discussed at any particular
moment.

Keith was more interested than his brothers or
his sister.  He was a lot more interested than
he was willing to let on.  He asked himself:

"Will they talk about my great-grandfather?  Was
he really a soldier in the Colonial Army?"

He patiently waited as each and every one of a
bunch of obscure cousins, aunts, and in-laws
were discussed.  He wanted to know about that
old man who had visited him all those times.
He began to become afraid they wouldn't talk
about his father's grand-daddy at all, but he
dared not ask.  One thing he didn't need was ri-
dicule about what his father called "Keith's
silly dreams."

Then, all of a sudden, he heard his aunt say:

"And, oh, I even found out some good stuff about
both Mother's and Daddy's parents."

Keith waited for what seemed like hours as Janet

went on and on about her and Ed's mother's family. Finally, she dug around in her bundle of papers and produced an envelope with the announcement:

"And here's some things about Daddy's family."

Keith almost forgot to breathe as she opened the envelope and took out some papers. Among these was a small portrait of an old-fashioned family. Janet pointed out a young man and explained that he was her and Ed's father as a young man.

Keith's eyes hurried past that boy's image to seek out the father of the family. There he stood, straight and tall in his Revolutionary War uniform. Keith had to fight back the tears that started to well up in his eyes. There, staring at the artist, was the same old man who had visited him in his room a few years earlier.

Janet was rambling on about how she had gotten all that information. By now Emily was aware that Keith had recognized his great-grandfather in that portrait. She saw that he was witnessing the proof of what he had seen and about which he had been chastised and ridiculed. She saw that he was on the verge of crying.

Emily turned to her sister-in-law and asked if she had the names of the people on the portrait.

"Yes, I do, here, on the back of the envelope."

Emily put her hand on that of Janet's and said:

"Tell us, what was Ed's grandfather's name? Did he have the initials L.T.L.?"

Janet hesitated a moment as she noted the intent look in Emily's eyes.  She turned the envelope over;

"Yes, here it is.  Our grandfather's name was Lewis Tallman Leaman."

# CHAPTER XXI

## THE SCHOOL TEACHER

his is one of those stories that we don't have very much information about. We don't know exactly where and when it happened.

It was understood by the source of this tale that it took place in or near Burlington. The best we have regarding the time is that it was a long long time ago, whatever that means.

It was on a Saturday and a small girl came home from play all excited about having met her teacher that afternoon in the woods near their house. It was in the fall and school had just been in session a few days, so the child was all enthused about being back in school. She liked her new teacher, the new classroom, and her new class.

She told her mother how the two of them had talked about school and that the teacher had told her what they would be studying that year. They talked about the child's pet dog

and how she hoped that her father would buy her
a pony cart for her birthday that was coming up
soon. As the child bubbled on and on about
their nice visit, her mother prepared the evening meal in readiness for the father to come
home.

The little girl was anxious for her father to
get home so she could tell him that she had
decided that she would be a schoolteacher when
she grew up.

She soon had her wish as she heard his familiar
footsteps on the porch. As they had their supper, the girl told him about the day in the
woods with her teacher. She told him of how the
teacher thought the pony cart was such a good
idea and how nice school was going to be.

The little girl's father shared the news of the
day with the two of them. An exchange of glances

unnoticed by the child also spoke of things
best left unsaid until she had gone to bed.

After the girl was safely tucked into her
bed, her father told his wife the really
big news of the day.  He told her of a fire
very early that morning in the boarding
house over by the school.  The damage to
the building wasn't serious, but two people
had been overcome by smoke and died.  One
of these was their little daughter's new
teacher.

# CHAPTER XXII

## MARCIA AND THE GYPSY

arcia Woodley was an exceptionally lovely young lady of fifteen the summer that the gypsies camped down along the creek below her parents' home between Danville and New London. Marcia, as well as her younger brother, Jason, had been given very strict orders not to go anywhere near that creek as long as the gypsies were there.

Their father's admonition that he wouldn't have to spank them if they did because the gypsies would steal them, thoroughly impressed young Jason. It scared Marcia, too. She sure didn't want to be kidnapped by a bunch of those strange people she had heard so much about.

Apparently, she wasn't scared enough, however. Her curiosity overcame her fear and off she went to see if she could get just a peek at the gypsies. Marcia wasn't nearly as discreet as she needed to be and was soon seen by one of the party camped there. A woman called to her by name. That left her momen-

tarily stunned. She was surprised that she
got caught. She was surprised that they
would call out to her, but to be called by
name was kind of a shock!

Shyly, Marcia walked up to the group as the
woman who called to her stepped out away from
the campfire to meet her. She was a friendly
appearing lady, not nearly as evil looking as
Marcia would have expected. In fact, the lady
looked much like any of the farm wives that
lived along the country road that she herself
lived on. The two introduced themselves and

engaged in small talk. Marcia soon found
herself much more at ease and was thinking
that these weren't such a mysterious people
after all.

As the young lady and the gypsy visited, the
cry of a baby came from a nearby tent. Marcia
asked if the baby was the lady's.

"In a way, it is."

"Can I see it?"

"Yes, come with me."

The pair entered the tent. There on a make-
shift bed was an almost new baby. As Marcia
began to lean over to see the infant, she
stood back up with a jerk. There on the
baby's knee was an L-shaped scar. It was
exactly the same shape and in the same spot
as one that she herself had. She had had
that scar all of her life as it was the result
of a serious injury at birth.

Marcia said, "It's really strange that both
the baby and I should have the same scar in
the same spot. You see, I have one just like
that on my knee."

"No," replied the lady. "It isn't strange at
all. You see she is you fifteen years ago and
I am you fifteen years hence."

With that, the lady uncovered her own knee.
There on the same spot was the same scar.

Bewildered and terrified, Marcia fled the
campsite and ran full tilt until she got
safely back to her own home. As she burst
into the house, her father knew that some-

thing was wrong. He demanded to know why she
had been running so, why she was so distraught,
and where had she been?

Between tears and sobs, Marcia told what had
happened down there in the gypsy camp by the
creek.

Marcia's father was both angry and confused.
He was upset that his daughter had deliber-
ately disobeyed him. He was angry at the
gypsies that had so terrified the poor girl.
He was at a loss to understand why that had
all happened and what it meant.

As he grabbed up a rifle, he shouted to his
wife to watch Jason and Marcia. Mr. Woodly
ran from the house and headed for the creek.
On the way he stopped to enlist the aid of
a neighbor and his good stout son.

The three men rushed down to the creek, Mr. Woodly explaining what had happened as they ran.

Within a few minutes, they got to the spot where they knew the gypsies had been camping. They found only the warm embers of a freshly abandoned campfire and a small white bootie with pink trim. They brought the bootie back to the Woodly home. It matched perfectly with the one that Marcia's mother had from when Marcia was a baby. The one that she had kept those fifteen years was the only one remaining of the original pair. Its mate had been lost for many years.

## CHAPTER XXIII

## HURON ISLAND

oday Huron Island is all but de-
serted. That was not always so.
Around the turn of the century,
there were several families living on the island. There were
even stores and a school. Most of the island's residents were farmers or fishermen.

Life on that island up at the northern end
of Des Moines County and out there in the
Mississippi River just sort of flowed along
like the big river it was so much a part of.
There was time to sit and relax.

So it was with George Moser. George enjoyed
many hours in drifting about in his small
boat among the backwaters in and around the
island. On several occasions he would take
one or more of his grandchildren with him,
if the water was calm. Drifting along, the
boat's occupants would talk and fish, or
just talk. It was a pleasant way to pass a
lazy summer afternoon.

This story is about the day that little Jenny
went with her grandfather. George had taken

Jenny out several times that summer. She
needed the companionship. She had lost her
little brother, Sammy, about a month earlier
in a drowning accident. Jenny missed him,
so George helped to keep her occupied.

It wasn't a fishin' type of afternoon. It
was just one of those driftin' and talkin'
kind of days. The sun was warm, yet not uncomfortable. Old George was almost half a-
sleep, just keeping one eye on Jenny as she

played with a string hung out over the side.
She was chattering along as only a ten-year-
old girl can do, when suddenly she dropped
silent.

This sudden quiet awakened George out of his
drowsiness to inquire as to what was wrong.

"Grandpa, there's nothing wrong at all. But
looky, there is Sammy's face down there deep
in the water."

Attempting to comfort the girl, George leaned

forward to take her hand. As he did so,
he glanced down into the water where Jenny
was looking. There were the unmistakable
features of Sammy Moser. Then the face
faded away and was gone.

That broke up that lazy summer afternoon.
George took his granddaughter home. Before he left that spot, however, he made
note of their exact location by dropping
a coin on a lily pad.

The next day he came back alone. He lo-
cated that spot and searched the water
for that image. Try as he might, he
couldn't find that face again.

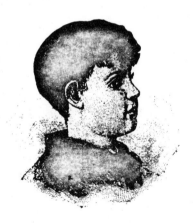

## CHAPTER XXIV

## THE FLOWER GIRL

o one seemed to have any idea
who she was. It was generally
thought that she must have been
the ghost of a girl who had
lived along Flint Creek. Every
time she was seen, it was somewhere along
that creek that flows out of the hills of
Des Moines County.

She was a pretty child. Why are ghost children always pretty? Aren't they ever plain,
or even homely?

She was always sighted in the spring or early
summer when the flowers are at their finest.
She would be among the flowers and either
picking them or carrying a bouquet of them.

The only report we have in which anyone ever
talked to the young lady was one in which a
woman walking into Burlington met her along
the road. The girl had a basket of blossoms
and was just standing in the shade of an oak
tree.

The lady, simply to make conversation, asked

the girl if she would sell her flowers.  The
girl replied:

"Why, yes."

With that she started to hand the lady her
bouquet.  As the lady reached out to take
them, the girl vanished and the flowers fell
to the ground.

The lady reported later that she found herself
standing there alone on the road in open-mouth-
ed amazement.  When she gathered her wits, she
looked down at those flowers lying in the dust.
Those fresh and pretty flowers lie brown and

lifeless as if they had been picked a month earlier.

The lady picked them up and the leaves and petals crumbled into a powder just as those will that have been pressed between the pages of a book for many years.

# EPILOGUE

So, what became of the little flower girl?
Who was she? Was she one of our neighbors
speaking to us in words we do not understand?

Did the little flower girl know of Kishauna's friend of Mediapolis or the girl
named Randy on South Hill of Burlington?

What of the Ghost of Highway #34? Did he
know Gustov "Pegleg" Nelson of Augusta, or
of The Old Brick Inn on Agency Road?

Perhaps there is a community of ghosts within our own, yet not of our own.

Whether we see them or not, or understand
them, or even believe in them, there are
those among us who reach out from time long
ago. They are the Lucindas of Stoney Hollow, the Andrew Neumans, the Marjories, and
Neil Simmons's solitary arm. They all stir
old memories, fire our imaginations, and
enrich our lives.

Deep within the soil of our beautiful Des
Moines County and in the depths of the Old

Mississippi River are secrets that we will never fully understand.

Perhaps we, by writing and by reading this book, can each touch the lives of those who have gone before us. Perhaps, in doing so, we can better understand our community and appreciate our heritage.

If this book has been of interest to you, perhaps you would also enjoy its companion, GHOSTS OF LEE COUNTY.

INDEX


Chapter titles are
shown in capital letters.

# INDEX

147

**Year**